Disney
The Further Adventures of

Aladdin

2 Birds of a Feather

BY A. R. Plumb

ILLUSTRATED BY
Laureen Burger
Mark Marderosian
H. R. Russell

Disney
PRESS
NEW YORK

Library of Congress Catalog Card Number: 94-71481
ISBN: 0-7868-4017-X
FIRST EDITION
1 3 5 7 9 10 8 6 4 2

Disney's

The Further Adventures of

Aladdin

2 Birds of a Feather

"Genie!" said Princess Jasmine. "You're just going away for a weekend and you packed a *hundred* suitcases?"

She looked around the throne room. Suitcases and trunks were piled everywhere.

"One hundred and forty-seven, to be exact. But who's counting?" The Genie sat down on a suitcase. He grunted and groaned and pounded. But it wouldn't close. "My clothes are packed in like sardines," he said.

The suitcase popped open and sent the Genie flying backward through the air. Inside were hundreds of little silver fish.

"Oops," said the Genie. "Looks like something fishy's going on in there."

Jasmine laughed. "You're just going to a genie convention. Take my advice. Pack light."

"Pack light. Hmm. Pack light." *Poof!* All the suitcases began to glow. Jasmine opened one. Inside were dozens of glowing lightbulbs.

The Genie looked embarrassed. "You know, ever since Al freed me, my powers aren't quite what they used to be."

For ten thousand years the Genie had been trapped in a magic lamp. But recently his friend Aladdin had set him free. Now he could come and go as he pleased, but his magic powers weren't quite as strong as they had been. He pointed at the suitcases again, and they stopped glowing.

Jasmine kissed the Genie on the cheek. "Well, your powers are still semiphenomenal and nearly cosmic. And that's good enough for me."

The Genie turned pink. Then red. Then redder. Then he turned himself into a bright red fire engine and zoomed around the room with his lights flashing. "Hey, Al," he called. "I think I'm in love."

Aladdin was sitting at a desk near the Sultan's throne. "Whatever you say," he said. He frowned at one of the pieces of paper in front of him.

"With *your* girlfriend," the Genie added teasingly.

"That's nice," Aladdin said.

Jasmine laughed. "Don't mind Aladdin," she told the Genie. "Father has a cold, so Aladdin is filling in for him today. I think he's a little nervous."

In the blink of an eye the Genie turned himself into a doctor in a white coat. He handed Jasmine a pot of chicken soup. "Tell the Sultan to eat two bowls of this and call me in the morning."

"Can't you just make Father well?" Jas-

mine asked.

"Hey, I'm good, but I'm not a miracle worker," said the Genie with a shrug. "Nobody can cure the common cold."

"Could you two be a little quieter over there?" Aladdin said, looking up from his papers. "I'm trying to concentrate."

"Sorry," said Jasmine. She lowered her voice. "Poor Aladdin. He's working on his speech for the dog show this afternoon. Since Father is sick, Aladdin volunteered to be the judge."

Zap! The Genie turned himself into a puffy little poodle. There were bows in his hair. His toenails were painted pink. He ran over to Aladdin and licked his cheek.

"Hey, big boy," Genie-the-dog said in a French accent. "Pick me! I can roll over. I can sit — "

"Yeah, but can you play dead?" Iago interrupted. The loudmouthed parrot was perched on Aladdin's shoulder.

"Sorry, Genie," said Aladdin. "No time to play."

The Genie ran back to Jasmine with his tail between his legs. "He *used to be* such a fun master," he said.

"Aladdin just wants to impress Father," Jasmine said. "Wait until you're back from your trip. Then Aladdin will be his old self again." She looked around. "Now, let's see if I can help you with all this luggage."

"Okay, but bear with me," said the Genie. Suddenly he turned into a huge black bear. He reached for a suitcase with his big paw. Sardines spilled out. The Genie tried to scoop them up. They popped out of his paw. One landed in Jasmine's hair.

"Man," said the Genie. "I'm all thumbs today!"

The Genie's paws grew five thumbs. He grabbed the sardines and stuffed them back into the suitcase.

"Sorry, Princess," said the Genie. He turned back into his real self. "I guess I'm just nervous about seeing my old genie buddies. I want to impress them — let them know I've hit the *big time*." He turned into a huge grandfather clock.

"Think of all the adventures we've had," said Jasmine. "You'll have plenty of amazing stories to tell the other genies."

The Genie's clock-face smiled. "I guess I have managed to do one or two interesting things. Although it takes a lot to impress genies."

Jasmine gave him a kind smile. "Just be yourself at the convention, Genie. Isn't that what you're always telling Aladdin?" She turned to leave. "Have a safe trip. . . . Oh, and Genie?"

"Yep?"

"Before you go, you might want to take that sardine out of your ear."

"How are you doing, Aladdin, my boy?"

Aladdin looked up from his speech. The Sultan had come into the throne room. His nose was red. He was wearing his favorite bathrobe and his bunny slippers. The magic flying carpet was with him.

"I'm doing my best," said Aladdin. "But I'm worried about the dog show, Sultan."

"It'll be easy," said the Sultan. He blew his nose. "Just tell the crowd how much you like dogs. Then put a blue ribbon on the cutest one. Nothing to it. Well, I'm off to try that soup the Genie whipped up."

Aladdin watched the Sultan leave. He picked up his speech. Slowly he began to read aloud.

"Citizens of Agrabah," he said. "Thank you for coming to the annual Desert Dog Show. We are here to honor man's best friend."

Someone made a gagging noise. Aladdin spun around. It was Abu. The little monkey was making a thumbs-down sign.

"I only said two lines!" Aladdin said.

"The furball has a point," said Iago. "It's that 'man's best friend' stuff. Who says dogs are man's best friend? You ever try talking to a dog? All you hear is *arf* this, *arf* that. Maybe a *ruff* or two. Face it. You want an intelligent conversation, get a bird. You want someone to slobber all over your face, get a dog."

Aladdin sighed. "You know, you guys really aren't helping." He tried again. "Citizens of Agrabah," he began.

Someone poked him in the ribs. It was Carpet. "*Now* what's wrong?" asked Aladdin.

Carpet put his tassels to his chest. He shook them. Then he bowed low.

"More gestures?" Aladdin asked. "Well, okay. If you say so." He continued reading. "We are here to honor man's best friend." Aladdin waved his arm. He waved his other arm. He felt ridiculous.

"Hold it. What was that? You trying to fly?" asked Iago. "You look like a real turkey. And you fly just about as well."

"Hey, this stuff isn't as easy as it looks," said Aladdin. "I'd like to see *you* try being sultan for a day. You've got it easy, Iago. Your biggest problem is deciding what to eat for breakfast."

"Easy? *Easy?*" Iago cried. "Do you know

what I have to put up with? Do you have any idea how I suffer?"

"Give me a break," said Aladdin. "All you do all day is flap your beak."

Iago glared at him. "Let me tell you about an average Iago day, Mr. Big Shot Sultan Stand-In. This morning I flew to my birdbath in the palace gardens. I was going to take a nice quiet dip. So I did a little parrot dive off a branch into the water." Iago pointed a wing at Abu. "But was it water I dove into, I ask you? *No!* It was lime green paint! That stupid chimp put *paint* in my birdbath!"

Abu started to laugh. He laughed so hard he fell to the ground. Tears rolled down his furry cheeks.

Iago couldn't stand it. He grabbed Abu's tail and tried to bite it. But Abu yanked his tail free just in time. Then he stuck out his tongue and scampered out of the throne room.

Aladdin tried very hard not to laugh. But he kept picturing a lime green Iago. Soon he was howling with laughter.

"Sure, laugh," said Iago grumpily. "*You* try getting green paint out of your tail feathers. Then see how hilarious it is. Oh, yes, it's real hilarious. I nearly passed out, I was laughing so hard."

"Sorry, Iago," said Aladdin when he managed to stop laughing. "But you have to admit it *is* kind of funny."

"I suppose you think being chased around by a mutant cat is funny, too?"

"You mean Rajah?" Aladdin asked. Rajah was Jasmine's pet tiger. His favorite game was chasing Iago.

"Of course I mean Rajah. That striped monster has it in for me."

"Oh, quit complaining," said Aladdin. He sat down at his desk. "That's just one cat. I have to deal with dozens of dogs this afternoon."

"You just don't know how to enjoy being sultan," said Iago. "If I were in your place, I'd be living it up. I'd lie back and let servants wait on me, wings and feet. Believe me, I'd give 'living in style' a whole new meaning."

"Then it's a good thing the Sultan asked me to help out and not you," Aladdin said.

Just then the Genie came over. "Well, I'm off," he said. "Knock 'em dead with your speech, kid."

"They'll die, all right," said Iago. "But

it'll be of boredom."

The Genie grabbed the large plaid suitcase he'd finally managed to squeeze everything into. Then he paused by the door and looked around. "Let's see," he said. "Suitcase? Check. Map? Check."

"Did you remember to turn off the stove?" asked Aladdin.

"Check," said the Genie. He scratched his chin. "Why do I feel like I'm forgetting something?"

Iago wasn't paying any attention to the Genie. "Yep," the parrot said. "I wish *I* were filling in for the Sultan. I wouldn't be wasting my time on dog shows. No sirree. You've got it made, kid. You're just too much of a nincompoop to know it."

Aladdin ignored the parrot. "Did you remember to pack extra underwear?" he called to the Genie.

"Check," the Genie said. "Purple polka dots. Always in style."

"Socks?"

"Check."

"Sunscreen?"

Iago gave a sigh. "Boy, I wish I had your life, kid."

Aladdin turned to the bird. "Hey, I'd give anything to trade places with *you* right now!" he said.

"Check," the Genie said.

"Uh-oh," said Iago.

The Genie headed out the door. "Farewell!" he called. "Good-bye! So long! Aloha! *Hasta la vista,* baby!"

Aladdin started to answer. But as soon as he opened his mouth, he had a bad feeling — a very bad feeling.

For one thing, he seemed to have grown a beak.

And for another thing, he seemed to be sprouting feathers.

"Genie!" Aladdin screamed. "Come back!"

Aladdin looked over at Iago. But he wasn't
Iago anymore. He was a tall boy with dark
hair and very wide eyes — a boy who
looked exactly like Aladdin.

Iago looked over at Aladdin. He wasn't
Aladdin anymore. He was a colorful parrot
with a big beak — a parrot who looked exactly like Iago.

"You're me!" Iago exclaimed.

"I'm not you — *squawk!* You're *me!*" Aladdin cried.

"Give me back my body!" Iago said.

"You give me back mine!" Aladdin said.

"This is all your fault!" Iago said.

"*MY* fault! You think I like being trapped in — *squawk!* — a suit of smelly bird feathers?"

"You're the wise guy who said you'd give anything to trade places with me," said Iago.

"I didn't really *mean* it," said Aladdin. "The Genie must have overheard me when he was leaving. He probably zapped us without knowing what he'd done."

"He's our only hope," said Iago. "We've got to catch him! He's got to switch us back before he leaves for his stupid convention."

Aladdin started to run, but his bird legs were too short.

"You're a bird, birdbrain," said Iago. "Use your wings."

Aladdin spread out his wings. He flapped. Nothing happened. He flapped

harder. Up, up, up — Aladdin was on his
way to the ceiling.

"I'm flying!" he said.

"That's a matter of opinion," said Iago.
"Flap harder."

Suddenly Aladdin lost speed. Down,
down, down — he did a nosedive into the
Sultan's throne.

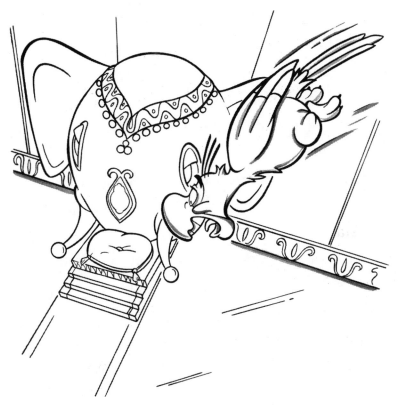

"You think that was bad," said Iago. "Wait until molting season. I can see I'm going to have to handle this. *I'll* go after that big blue bozo."

Iago began running. There was just one problem — he tried to move both legs at the same time. He tripped and rolled over twice. When he tried to stand up, he tripped again.

"One leg at a — *squawk!* — time," Aladdin said.

"Great," said Iago. "At this rate we'll never get out of here. The Genie's probably long gone by now."

Carpet whooshed over to Aladdin. Aladdin hopped on board. "Thanks, Carpet," he said.

Carpet picked up Iago next. Iago stumbled slightly on his strange legs. "Let's go, rug," he ordered.

They sped out of the throne room. Around the corner, through the doors, and

past the guards they went. Carpet stopped on the front steps of the palace and looked around for any sign of the Genie.

"Genie!" Aladdin called out. But there was no answer. "*Now* what are we going to do?" he asked. "We'll never be able to — *squawk!* — catch up with him!"

"Will you quit that squawking already?" Iago said. "It's embarrassing. I haven't squawked like that since I was a chick."

"I can't — *squawk!* — help it," Aladdin said.

"Well, work on it," Iago said. "After all, people are going to think you're me."

"And people will think *you're* me!" Aladdin said.

"What a terrible situation this — " Suddenly Iago paused. He smiled broadly. "Being *you* does present certain possibilities," he mused. "Very interesting possibilities."

"I don't like the sound of that," said

Aladdin. Carpet nodded.

Iago rubbed his new human hands together. "I'm stuck being you until the Genie comes back. And you're in charge until the Sultan gets better." He cleared his throat and continued, in a perfect imitation of Aladdin's voice, "What does all this mean?"

"This means you're — *squawk!* — going to get me in a whole lot of trouble," said

Aladdin. He tried to shake a finger at Iago. But he'd forgotten he didn't have fingers anymore. He shook a wing instead. Carpet shook a tassel.

"Outta my way, kid," said Iago. "Or should I say *bird*? I think I'm going to enjoy being sultan for a day."

Just then Rajah wandered up. He looked from Aladdin to Iago and back again.

Aladdin held out a wing. "Rajah! It's me, Aladdin. Trust me — *squawk!*"

Rajah cocked his head. He looked very confused.

Iago stroked the tiger's head. "Hey, kitty-

kitty," he said in Aladdin's voice. "Why don't you go play chase with the nice little birdie?"

Rajah's golden eyes lit up. He growled at Aladdin and licked his chops. Now that Aladdin was much smaller, the tiger's teeth suddenly seemed *much* larger.

"No!" Aladdin cried. *"He's* Iago!"

But it was too late. Rajah charged at Aladdin. Aladdin flapped his wings. He made it a few feet off the ground.

"Now we'll see who has an easy life!" said Iago.

But Aladdin couldn't answer. He was much too busy trying not to get eaten.

Aladdin flew as fast as he could. By the time he reached the palace gardens, he was very tired. And Rajah was still right behind him.

Aladdin spied a high branch on a palm tree. It looked like the perfect place to rest. Even Rajah would have a hard time climbing that high. No wonder it was Iago's favorite spot to nap.

Aladdin landed on the branch. His wings ached. Being a bird was harder than it looked.

Rajah lay down at the base of the tree

and waited. Aladdin sighed. "The first thing I need to do is find Abu and Jasmine," he told himself. "They'll know it's me — even if Rajah can't tell."

A scary thought hit him. He gulped. What if Abu and Jasmine *didn't* know who he was? What if Aladdin couldn't convince them that he and Iago had switched bodies? After all, Iago could do a perfect imitation of almost any voice. He'd have no trouble sounding just like Aladdin. And when the others heard Aladdin's voice coming out of Iago's body, they'd probably just think the parrot was playing a trick on them by pretending to be Aladdin.

Then an even scarier thought hit him. What if the Genie couldn't switch them back? His powers weren't as strong as they used to be. What if Aladdin had to stay a bird forever? No more seeing the world. No more adventures with Jasmine. No more helping the Sultan.

He heard a noise and looked down. Abu was coming toward him, carrying a bamboo stick and a piece of paper.

"Abu!" Aladdin cried. "Little buddy! It's me, Aladdin!"

Abu stopped at the bottom of the tree. He looked up. Then he looked at Rajah. Rajah shrugged.

"I switched bodies with Iago," Aladdin said. "The Genie did it by mistake."

Abu rolled his eyes and started to laugh. Rajah looked amused.

"It's not funny," Aladdin said. "I'm serious, Abu! Please go find Jasmine."

Abu tore off a piece of paper and rolled it into a little ball. Then he put it into his mouth.

"No, not a spit wad!" Aladdin cried. He knew Abu was an excellent shot. He knew because he was the one who had taught Abu how to shoot spit wads.

Abu put the paper ball into the end of

the hollow bamboo stick. He blew hard.
The spit wad flew into the air. It hit Aladdin in the beak.

It didn't hurt — but it was gross.

Abu began to laugh again. Rajah grinned
broadly. "That does it!" said Aladdin. "If
you won't believe me, Jasmine will!" He
flapped his wings. But something was
wrong. He couldn't take off.

Abu laughed even harder. He pointed to
Aladdin's feet.

Aladdin looked down. He tried to move
one foot. It wouldn't budge. He tried to

move the other foot. Then he noticed something. White gooey stuff covered the top of the branch.

"Glue!" Aladdin cried.

Abu nodded proudly. He and Rajah grinned at one another.

"But I'm *not* Iago!" Aladdin said again. "You've got to trust me, Abu—*squawk!*"

But Abu just made another spit wad and aimed at Aladdin.

Whoosh! Out of the palace came Carpet. He soared up to Aladdin. Carpet shook a tassel at Abu to scold him. He put another tassel around Aladdin and started to help him detach his feet from the branch.

"Thanks," said Aladdin. "I'm glad you're here. Abu doesn't believe it's me." He scratched at an itchy spot on his wing. Looking down, he saw a splotch of lime green paint. He sighed. He was starting to think that maybe Iago did have a tough life, after all.

"Where *is* Aladdin?" asked Jasmine.

She looked into the gardens. Iago was high up in a tree with Carpet. Rajah and Abu sat at the foot of the tree. But Aladdin wasn't with them.

Jasmine headed to the reflecting pool. She'd looked all over the palace for Aladdin. Where could he be? It was almost time to leave for the dog show.

When she reached the reflecting pool, Jasmine's mouth dropped open. Aladdin was lying on a raft in the middle of the pool. One servant was shading him with an umbrella. Another one was holding a bowl of food for him to eat. A third servant was playing a small harp and singing softly.

But that wasn't all. Aladdin was wearing new clothes of the finest gold cloth. He had a ring on every finger. His gold turban had a huge ruby on it.

"Aladdin!" Jasmine said. "Where are your old clothes?"

"Those rags?" Aladdin said. "I had them burned. Today I'm the sultan, Jasmine. Don't you think I should look the part?" He opened his mouth and pointed. One of the servants dropped a piece of food into it.

"What are you eating?" Jasmine asked.

"Sunflower seeds," said Aladdin. "I had a sudden craving."

"I guess you must have finished your speech."

"What speech?" Aladdin frowned. "Oh, you mean for that doggie duel? I'm skipping that shindig."

"But Father is counting on you!"

"Come on, Princess. You've seen one mutt, you've seen them all." He made a face. "Dogs! I can't stand the beasts. Filthy, smelly animals. Way too many teeth."

"Aladdin, you *have* to judge the dog show," Jasmine cried. She couldn't understand what was wrong with him. It just wasn't like Aladdin to be so irresponsible.

"Look, for the time being, I'm sultan. That means what I say goes, right? And I say I'm going to enjoy myself." Aladdin held up a foot. "What would you think about having some matching gold slippers made?"

"I'd say I can't believe how you're acting!" Jasmine cried.

"Silver?" Aladdin asked.

Jasmine tapped her foot. "You wanted to prove to Father how responsible you could be. And now look at you! You're lying around while other people wait on you."

"Yep," said Aladdin. "Just like him. I'm a chip off the old blockhead." He patted his stomach. "Of course, the old blockhead's a lot bigger around the middle."

"What is the matter with you?" Jasmine demanded angrily. "One minute you're working hard, the next minute you're lazy and selfish and obnoxious. You might as well be Iago!"

"Hey, he's not such a bad guy," said Aladdin. "He's just misunderstood. Would you like a sunflower seed?"

"I give up!" Jasmine cried. "If you won't judge the dog show, I will."

Jasmine stomped off toward the palace.

She was near the door when she heard someone call her name.

She turned. Iago was flying over. He wasn't flying very well, though. He kept dragging his tail feathers along the ground. And he landed face first on the ground in front of her. Carpet flew over to help. It took him three tries to pull Iago's beak out of the ground.

"Nice landing," said Jasmine.

Iago wiped dirt off his beak. "We need to talk."

The parrot's voice sounded funny, but Jasmine didn't have time to worry about that. "I'm busy, Iago," Jasmine said. "Aladdin's acting very strange —"

"That's not Aladdin," said Iago. "*I'm* Aladdin!"

Jasmine laughed. It was a crazy story — just the kind of story Iago would make up. "*You're* Aladdin?" So that explained the strange voice. Iago was imitating Aladdin, probably as part of some kind of weird practical joke.

"Exactly! I'm so relieved — *squawk!* — that you believe me," the parrot said.

"Of course I believe you," Jasmine said with a giggle. "Why wouldn't I believe you're Aladdin? So what if you have feathers and a beak and wings?"

"But it's true! The Genie did it. It was

an accident."

Jasmine thought for a moment. The Genie *had* been very distracted today. And Aladdin *was* acting pretty strange. Then Jasmine shook her head. No, that was silly. Why would the Genie turn Aladdin into Iago?

"Nice try, Iago," Jasmine said. "But I'm not falling for it." She started to walk away.

"Wait!" the parrot cried. "Wait. I can prove I'm — *squawk!* — Aladdin."

"I know something Iago could never know," the parrot continued.

"There are a *lot* of things Iago doesn't know," Jasmine said.

"But this is about you and me," the little bird replied. He fluttered up to Jasmine's shoulder. "Remember the first time I took you for a ride on Carpet? We saw pagodas and pyramids. Stars and seas. We flew through an apple orchard, and I grabbed an apple for you." The parrot sighed. "And

when we got back to the palace —*squawk!*—
something wonderful happened."

"Our first kiss," Jasmine whispered. She
looked deep into the parrot's eyes. "Aladdin! It really *is* you in there!"

"Boy, am I glad you finally believe me," Aladdin said. "I was starting to think I'd never convince you."

Jasmine began pacing. "Now all we have to do is figure out how to switch you back — and quickly." She snapped her fingers. "Carpet, I want you to find that convention. Tell the Genie what's happened."

"Good luck trying to explain *this* mess," Aladdin said.

"Bring him back here as fast as you can," Jasmine said.

Carpet saluted Jasmine. Before they

could even say good-bye, he was zipping through the skies.

"Next we have to deal with the dog show," said Jasmine.

"You're not going to say *I* should judge it, are you?" asked Aladdin. "I'm sure those dogs—*squawk!*—would love a parrot snack."

Jasmine shook her head. "Come on," she said. "We're going to go have a talk with Iago."

On their way to the reflecting pool, they passed Rajah and Abu. They were dozing in the sun under a coconut tree.

"Wake up, you two!" said Jasmine. "I have an announcement to make."

Abu yawned. When he saw the parrot perched on Jasmine's shoulder, he grabbed his bamboo shooter. Rajah growled.

"No, no!" said Jasmine. "I know this *looks* like Iago. But it really is Aladdin. The Genie made them trade bodies by mistake."

Abu's eyes went wide. He jumped onto
Jasmine's other shoulder and began to
chatter loudly at Aladdin, looking worried.
Rajah covered his head with his paws.

"I accept your apology, Abu," said Aladdin. "And yours, too, Rajah." He laughed.
"By the way, your aim's improved, Abu. I
don't think you missed once with those spit
wads!"

"Come on," said Jasmine. "We have
work to do."

They found Iago at the reflecting pool. He was still on his raft. One of the servants was giving him a manicure.

Iago frowned when he saw Aladdin perched on Jasmine's shoulder. "What are you doing with that parrot?" Iago asked in Aladdin's voice.

"Jasmine knows the — *squawk!* — truth," said Aladdin. He pointed a wing at Iago. "She knows who you *really* are."

"What's that birdbrain squawking about?" Iago said.

"That birdbrain is really Aladdin," said Jasmine. "There's no use pretending, Iago."

Iago kicked the manicurist out of the way and stood up. "Okay," he said in his own voice. He crossed his arms over his chest. "So we switched bodies. The Genie screwed up — as usual. The truth is, I'm enjoying myself here." He waved an arm at the servants who were waiting on him.

"Don't get too used to it," said Aladdin.

"Carpet's gone to get the Genie."

"Well, until he gets back, I'm you. And you're me. And there's nothing you can do about it," said Iago. He lay back on his raft and crossed his arms behind his head. "I'm going to enjoy being sultan while I can."

"Then you'd better get over to the dog show," said Jasmine. "Because that's where the sultan is supposed to be right now."

"And why would I do that when I can

stay right here and have my every wish granted?"

"Because soon the Genie's going to put you back in your parrot body," said Jasmine. "And after I tell Father what happened, he may just decide to put you on a diet of crackers and water — for a *very* long time. That is, unless you decide to help."

Iago frowned and thought about that for a minute. He hated crackers. And he knew Jasmine was the type to carry out her threats. "I am not a helpful guy, you know." He climbed off his raft again. "That's one thing nobody's ever accused me of. As a matter of fact, I *hate* helpful guys."

Jasmine gave him a warning look.

"But as a favor to you," Iago said quickly, "I'll go to the dog show."

"I thought you might," said Jasmine. "Let's go. The camels are waiting to take us to the marketplace." She patted Rajah on the head. "You'd better stay here. Cats and dogs don't mix."

Iago looked at Aladdin. "I wouldn't come along if I were you," he said. "Birds and dogs don't mix either."

Aladdin laughed. "If things go wrong, I'll just fly away."

"You're a braver bird than I am," said Iago. "I mean, *was*."

By the time Jasmine, Aladdin, Iago, and
Abu reached the marketplace, it was filled
with people and dogs. There were big dogs
and little dogs, fat dogs and skinny dogs,
cute dogs and ugly dogs.

"Have you ever seen so many mutts in
one place in your life?" asked Iago.

A big black dog with long ears ran up to
Aladdin and sniffed at him curiously. "Nice
pooch — *squawk!*" said Aladdin.

The dog began to growl.

"I told you birds and dogs don't mix," said Iago.

Aladdin flapped his wings. The dog lunged for him. Aladdin made it up to Jasmine's shoulder and perched there.

"I hope you don't mind, Jasmine," he said. "I feel safer up here."

Jasmine led them to the center of the marketplace, where a large platform had been erected. "That's where you'll judge the dogs," Jasmine told Iago.

"This is not a good idea, people," said Iago, who was still glancing around nervously at all the dogs. "I am telling you this is definitely going down in history as a not-good idea." He wrung his hands. "I have this thing about dogs."

"What kind of thing?" Aladdin asked.

"Dogs and I, we have a kind of understanding," said Iago. "I hate them. They hate me."

"I wish the Genie were here," said Aladdin. "Then I could judge the show. And you'd be wearing these smelly feathers."

"Hey, birdboy," said Iago. "My feathers do *not* smell. Besides, you should be glad to have my wings. I wish *I* had my wings back! I'm telling you, this walking business is starting to get on my nerves. How do you people ever get anywhere on time?" He held out a leg. "Talk about slow going!"

Jasmine cleared her throat. "Come on, you two. We'll just have to hope the Genie gets here soon."

She climbed up onto the platform. The others sat down on chairs. The crowd hushed. Even the dogs were quiet. "Citizens of Agrabah," Jasmine said. "I am sorry to report that the Sultan has taken ill with a cold. He has asked his most trusted adviser to fill in for him. I am proud to introduce you to my good friend Aladdin."

The crowd applauded and whistled. Iago

just sat there. Jasmine gave him a nudge with her foot.

"Oh. I forgot who I was," said Iago. "I mean, *am*."

"Don't forget to talk like Aladdin," Jasmine hissed. Then she sat down, and Iago stepped up to the podium.

The crowd watched Iago eagerly, waiting to hear him speak.

"What can I say about dogs?" he said at last with a shrug. "They're big. They're stupid. They eat smelly dead things."

People gasped. A large white dog near the platform growled.

"Face it, folks," said Iago. "What other animal is dumb enough to fetch on command? Or chase its tail for three hours straight? You won't catch a bird doing that kind of thing. Hey, did you hear the one about the beagle and the bald eagle?"

Jasmine put her head in her hands. This was not going well. She ran over to Iago.

"Here," she said. She handed him the ribbons for the winning dogs. "Why don't you quit while you're behind?"

Iago took the ribbons. "Okay, pooches," he said. "Line up. Show me your stuff. Impress me." He rolled his eyes. "Yeah, right," he muttered. "Like I'm going to be wowed by some bowwow."

The dogs all lined up in a row in front of Iago. Jasmine sighed and glanced at Aladdin, who was still perched on her shoulder. A few more minutes and this would be over. She crossed her fingers.

Just then she felt someone tap her other shoulder. "Sorry I'm late, Princess. We ran into a lot of air traffic."

She and Aladdin turned around. The Genie and Carpet were standing behind the platform, hidden from the crowd.

"Genie!" Aladdin exclaimed. "I've never —*squawk!*— been so happy to see anyone!"

"I'm really sorry about the mix-up, Al."
The Genie hung his head. "I feel so small."

Poof! The Genie shrank down to the size
of a thumbnail.

"It wasn't so bad," said Aladdin. "I
learned how to fly." He smiled. "Of course,
I'm no Carpet." Carpet gave a modest bow.
"But I did get off the ground."

The Genie returned to normal size. "Well
it's just a matter of a little hocus-pocus. I'll

have you reunited with your old body in a jiff."

On the platform, Iago waved a shiny blue ribbon. "And now, for the moment you've all been waiting for," he said.

He pointed to a very large, very mean-looking dog. The dog had razor-sharp white teeth. And he looked as though he had a very healthy appetite.

"First place goes to the big guy with the excellent dental work," said Iago.

"Personally, I was rooting for the poodle with the beehive hairdo," the Genie said. He turned to Aladdin. "Now, let's do something about *your* do. The feather look just isn't working for me."

"No, Genie!" Jasmine cried. "Not now —"

Zap! Aladdin jumped off Jasmine's shoulder just in time to avoid crushing her as he returned to his normal shape and size. He landed on the ground with a thump.

At the same moment Iago shrank back to

his old parrot self. He clutched the blue ribbon under his wing.

The crowd gasped. The dogs snarled.

Aladdin stood up. "I've never been so glad to be me," he said to Jasmine. "Or so glad *not* to be Iago."

The dog grabbed his blue ribbon between his teeth. "Attaboy, Rover," said Iago. The parrot took a step back.

The dog chewed and swallowed the ribbon.

"Nice puppy," said Iago. He took another step back.

The dog snapped at Iago.

"Down, boy," Iago said. "Down, you four-legged monstrosity."

The dog leaped at Iago. Iago flapped his wings, and the chase was on. The dog's mouth was just inches from Iago's tail feathers.

"Hey, get this mutt off me!" Iago yelled as he flew around the marketplace in circles. "Guys? Come on! Save me, will you?"

"Should I save him?" the Genie asked Aladdin and Jasmine.

Jasmine and Aladdin looked at each other.

"Oh, I suppose you'll have to," Aladdin said at last.

"Of course," Jasmine added, "there's no hurry!"